THE Last Rose OF Autumn

VOLUME 1
In the Fullness of Time

By
DEBBIE WELLS NOBIS

Copyright © 2013 by Debbie Wells Nobis

The Last Rose of Autumn
by Debbie Wells Nobis

Printed in the United States of America

ISBN 9781626977600

All rights reserved solely by the author. The author guarantees all contents are original and do not infringe upon the legal rights of any other person or work. No part of this book may be reproduced in any form without the permission of the author. The views expressed in this book are not necessarily those of the publisher.

Unless otherwise indicated, Bible quotations are taken from the New King James Version (NKJV). Copyright © 1982 by Thomas Nelson, Inc. Used by permission. All rights reserved.

All songs quoted are taken from The Modern Hymnal, copyright © 1926, by Robert H. Coleman, Dallas TX

www.xulonpress.com

Many thanks to Audra and Gail who read for me.

And special thanks to my nephew,
Michael, who helped edit.

I love you guys.

Foreword

The last rose of autumn blooms after the summer heat and before winter frost at a time when you think it's too late for new life to begin. It's as if everything that is good and fragrant is poured into one precious flower for God's praise and glory.

The last rose of autumn, it's you and it's me.

Table of Contents

Foreword v

Mr. Henry 9

Emma Has a Day Job 19

Nothing 25

A Funny Thing Happened Today 31

Birdhouses. 37

A Shirt for Joe 51

Escape from Gomorrah 56

Something Pretty. 74

You Can't Take it with You 81

Ohio Blue Tip 94

Reference 100

Mr. Henry

On the winding road between Chesney and Dirksy stands the farmhouse where Mr. Henry Widmoor lived. Mr. Henry was an ordinary-looking man, small of stature and trim of frame, but he was blessed with an air of dignity and confidence that imbued people with a deep respect for him. His wife had passed away, and if he had any other relatives, nobody knew of them. He was a reserved man who worked hard, and although he was always polite, he pretty much kept to himself.

As Mr. Henry increased in age, he gradually rented out more and more of his farmland until all he retained for himself was the small acreage around his house. The farm work that had filled his days had also kept him company, so with retirement came loneliness. After the first idle winter, the days of spring brought Mr. Henry out of his house with a plan. Carefully, piece by piece, he selected a collection of machinery parts from the discarded

The Last Rose of Autumn

farm implements behind his barn. He welded them together in an interesting way, braised and polished his creation, and set it in his front yard next to a bright "For Sale" sign and awaited events.

Soon, people began stopping by to ask what it was. They would walk around the assemblage, pointing out parts they recognized and speculate about others, while enjoying a visit with Mr. Henry and satisfying their curiosity.

Word of Mr. Henry's Odyssey spread and people from the city began to drive out to see this *objet d'art*. Frankly, most of them would not have known a hay rake from a milk separator, but they would gaze intently at Mr. Henry's creation, critique his work, and speculate about its meaning. Mr. Henry would nod and smile and keep his thoughts to himself.

One of the visitors who came was an artsy young fellow from the university who had heard of Mr. Henry's fine craftsmanship. He admired the work very much, but he did not bore Mr. Henry by talking about composition or lines, light and shadow, or how his art translated to the deeper meaning of life. He appreciated Mr. Henry's art, but it was the science that he found intriguing.

Mr. Henry invited the visitor to his workshop and showed him the other pieces he was working on. His guest was fascinated. "How do you do that?" he asked with a sincere hunger. "How do you know which parts to choose, and how do you make them appear to float in mid-air and *move?*"

Mr. Henry

The old man's heart warmed and he knew he had met a kindred spirit, so he explained: "I can teach you to weld and braise the pieces together, that's simply knowledge and practice. It's the Lord who gives me the inspiration for which cogs and gears and parts to select and how to put them together then polish them in a way that teases the eye and touches the soul."

A cynical look marred the young man's face and the contemptuous curl of his lip told Mr. Henry that his guest did not believe in God. He was a man educated in science and numbers, and he was a man whom life had taught to cultivate a hard heart, but Mr. Henry was not rebuffed.

"I can see you don't believe in God," he observed with gentle understanding.

"I believe in science," was the young man's stony reply.

"Oh, God loves science! The Father delights in giving His children a puzzle to solve or unfathomable beauty to admire. Wonders like the Aurora Borealis and fireflies, butterflies! Oh yes," he mused deeply reverent, "God loves science."

The young man was not moved.

"Well, it took me a long time to get acquainted with Him," acknowledged Mr. Henry prosaically, "so let's you and me work on welding and leave the rest to God, shall we?"

The young man agreed and they began to work together but as friends, not as teacher and student.

Each learned from the other, neither so pot-sure of himself that he didn't have room in his mind for a better way or a new technique, and they became close friends.

During their time together, Mr. Henry would often quote Scripture or sing hymns while he worked or as he paused to wait on the Lord for inspiration; although the young man did not share them, he was respectful of Mr. Henry's beliefs.

One day Mr. Henry asked his friend if he knew any Scripture verses and the young man replied that "spare the rod and spoil the child" was the only verse he remembered hearing, and he had never grown to appreciate it.

"That's a shame, I've always thought that verse was misunderstood. David said 'Thy rod and thy staff comfort me.' It's not likely that a father who said that would strike his children. David was a shepherd, so I've always thought his son, Solomon, meant that parents should guide their children not hit them, but that's just my opinion. You seem very fond of your boys and I'm thinking you will be more of an Ephesians 6:4 parent to your little ones."

The young man agreed that it was better "*not to provoke your children to wrath*" but privately doubted he would ever encourage his boys to "*live in the nurture and admonition of the Lord*".

As time does, it slipped by and they enjoyed their visits together for many months; then one day the young man went to the farm and they did not work. Mr. Henry was weary and the wind was sharp making it too chilly for the old man to be out in the drafty workshop; so they sat at the kitchen table drinking tea and eating marshmallow cookies as they talked the afternoon away. To the young man, it seemed that Mr. Henry was exceptionally poignant as he shared the important moments in his life: the mistakes he had made, the lessons he had learned, and the victories that had been a long time coming. He seemed to be pouring out all he had stored up, and with humble wisdom, the young man asked questions and intuitively schooled his mind to remember every detail of the day.

A few evenings later, Mr. Henry's pastor called the young man to tell him that the old gent had passed away; and to ask him, as Mr. Henry's closest friend, if he would go to the farm and make sure the house and outbuildings were locked up properly.

The young man was stunned. Without realizing it, Mr. Henry *had* become his closest friend.

He drove to the house without shedding a tear, then he opened the back door and stepped into the kitchen. Waves of nostalgia overwhelmed him and he looked around the comfortable room feeling perfectly at home but completely lost. It was the emptiness, the knowing that his friend would not be coming back that broke him and he shook with deep racking sobs.

His life was a mess. His wife had moved out taking the children with her, his position at the college was in danger, and his soul was in turmoil. And now, the man who had become the anchor of his life was gone too. Despair gripped him and he whispered fearfully:

"Mr. Henry's god? Are...are you here, sir? Please! Tell me where you are. Are you here? Are you here, sir?"

Silence answered him. He looked around the room trying to figure out where God would be and his eyes fell on the chair where Mr. Henry had knelt to pray. The old man had spent so much time there that the linoleum flooring had two deeply worn places where his knees had rested. The young man went to the chair hoping for something mystical that would bring him closer to God. He looked around desperate for a sign. Finding none, he cried out like a lost child:

"Mr. Henry's god! Please! Show me that you *are* real. Is this the place, sir? Is this where you are? *Mr. Henry's god! Help me! Please!*"

And he dropped to his knees and wept until he had no more tears.

He mourned his friend, his misspent life, his troubled marriage, and his foolish beliefs; most of all, he mourned the connection he had begun to feel with God through his friendship with Mr. Henry. Then an odd thing happened as he wept, a peace he had never known began to grow in his heart, and he was moved to speak words he never thought he would say.

He forgave his father for the mean way he had acted and the harsh words he had spoken. He forgave his wife for wanting more than he could give her finally understanding she did not want another man, she yearned for a spiritual connection to a higher power. He acknowledged that the coworker who wanted his job was just trying to get ahead and provide for his family, and forgave his competitor for harboring the same ambition that blinded him. And he forgave himself for having been so afraid of being disappointed that he could not see what God had been trying to give him.

He wiped his face with his sleeve and sat on the floor gently rubbing his hand back and forth in the grooves left by his old friend's knees. These were Mr. Henry's grooves worn into the floor by years of worship and prayer, and he knew he had to make his *own* grooves and asked God to show him how.

Carefully aligning his knees with the marks left by his spiritual father, the young man knelt and told God he was sorry for the things he had done and for not believing in Him. And he asked Jesus to come into his life and be his lord and savior. "Help me, please Sir. Help me understand how to do this because I don't have a clue and I'm not nearly as smart as I thought I was."

When he got up, he saw Mr. Henry's Bible laying open on the kitchen table and went to see what page it was opened to. It was Philippians and he was drawn to 2:12 where the last part of the passage had

The Last Rose of Autumn

been underlined by an unsteady hand "*... work out your own salvation with fear and trembling*".

Mr. Henry had told him that. He had told him we all work out our own salvation with fear and trembling. It was his time now and he was ready to work out his own relationship with God. Tomorrow he would come back and clean out the refrigerator and check the water pipes, tonight he had other things to do.

He went outside and laid the Bible on the front seat of his car, but before he could leave, the workshop had to be checked. As he pulled the chain on the old green shop-light that hung over the worktable, the project he had been working on beckoned. It was welded together, ready and waiting to be finished. All the parts were there, but it had no life. It had resisted and stymied him. He could not figure out how to make the parts appear to move the way Mr. Henry could.

Then he remembered his friend's instructions, took a deep breath and said: "Mr. Henry's god, m... my God, what do I do with this now?" and he expectantly picked up a piece of emery cloth and waited for direction.

A vision formed in his head and his hands began to work. He didn't think, he didn't design, he just copied what he saw in his head. Twenty minutes later, he stepped back and looked at what the Lord had shown him. The beauty of the piece staggered him and an inner voice told him to turn off the

Mr. Henry

manmade light. He pulled the chain and as the glow of moonlight coming through the skylight washed the room with whiteness, the sculpture jumped to life. He walked around the piece and shivered as the gears and wheels appeared to whirl. He was so convinced they were moving that he had to touch them, and even then, he questioned his fingers.

His heart sang and he threw back his head and laughed. He was right! Wise, wonderful, believing Mr. Henry was right! God did have the answer. It felt like a miracle and the young man was not ready to stop there. He dropped to his knees and spoke to God again, this time with growing courage:

"Sir, would You please fix my marriage and show me how to be the husband and father Mr. Henry said You want me to be? It's the *more* I'm asking for, Sir. Jesus said: '*This and more will you do in my name*', I *was* listening, Sir, when Mr. Henry talked, I was listening, and he always asked in Jesus name, so I am too. In Jesus name, Sir, please, teach me to be a better man."

With that he locked the door and drove back to the city heading straight to the apartment where his wife was staying. He was not sure she would talk to him or even answer the door, but he knew he had to try so he knocked and waited.

He saw the light flicker in the security peep-hole then the bolt clicked and the door opened. She looked sad and tired and did not speak. She just stood there

The Last Rose of Autumn

looking at him not knowing whether to be actively hostile or merely defensive.

"I've been a terrible fool," he said melting her heart, "but I've got this great book that covers life and marriage and parenting, and I'm wondering if you would be willing to study it with me."

He held out Mr. Henry's Bible and his stunned wife laughed and cried as she laid her hand on the book she had been deeply longing to share with her husband. A deep sigh of relief escaped him and he gently laid his thumb over hers silently thanking God and earnestly thinking that this prayer thing was something he wanted to know a lot more about.

Emma Has a Day Job

*E*mma was a smallish black lab with a kind heart and an amazing capacity to love. For most of her life, she lived at an old two-story house that sat on ten acres between a city and a small town. She liked it there. Her days were filled with the kind of adventures dogs enjoy, and the man who had adopted her never tied her up and rarely scolded her. She liked him too.

The man worked out of an office in the house and every morning he would make coffee, feed Emma, then go outside and sit on an old bench under a large silver maple tree and talk to God. Emma was not very good with words but she truly understood emotions, and she knew in her heart that the man was good and that his love for God was real. Dogs are smart that way.

She learned to be patient while the man prayed and she would sit next to him or lie on the bench with her head in his lap. When he finished, he would play

The Last Rose of Autumn

with her for a while then say: "Time to go to work," and he would go in the house and Emma would trot down the long lane to the black-top road and not be seen again until late in the afternoon.

When people asked where she went, the man would jokingly reply: "Emma has a day job."

He would laugh and explain that somebody else in the neighborhood probably thought Emma was their dog too, and maybe she was, her heart was certainly big enough to love lots of people.

To be honest, the man was pretty laid back and didn't care where Emma went as long as she was not bothering anyone, but when his usually trim dog began to get fat he wondered why. He knew what it wasn't, he just didn't know what it was. So to satisfy his curiosity, one morning when Emma trotted down the driveway, he went with her. She was thrilled with his company and would joyfully frisk around him then lope off to investigate something and come running back to him. As they walked, he watched with great interest as she went from house to house heading straight for water bowls and food dishes apparently set out for her. And at houses where the owners were home, Emma was greeted with warm affection and a treat.

Everyone loved her. Even the elderly neighbor who shooed Emma out of her yard seemed pleased to see her in spite of scowling at the man and demanding: "Is this your dog, young man?"

Emma Has a Day Job

Gray haired and a grandfather, he admirably hid the smile that made his mustache twitch. He acknowledged the connection and asked apologetically if Emma had been a nuisance.

The woman had hesitated. "Well, no, she's not a pest. In fact she's my most constant visitor. No matter how many times I chase her away, she keeps coming back. I wish my family was as resilient," she added wistfully.

As they walked on, the man had smiled at Emma and leaned down to scratch her ear. "I'm proud of you."

After that, the man thought very little about Emma's avocation. Neighbors around them moved out and new people moved in, and if Emma wanted to befriend them, that was her business. He was content that she came home to him every night and that she loved him the most.

Life was good. Emma and the man continued to get along very well, and on the weekends, the man's grandchildren would come to visit and they would play and have lots of fun. Then one spring, the man was gone a little more than normal, and sometimes, a lady about his age would come to visit. They would fix food and take the cd player outside so they could watch the sunset and dance on the patio.

Emma liked The Dancing Lady. She was good at petting, could always be counted on to pull off a tick, and frequently got around the "don't feed the dog table scraps" rule by carelessly letting choice

The Last Rose of Autumn

bits of meat fall on the ground. She was thoughtful that way, but what Emma liked best was when the lady came early on Sunday morning. The man never locked his house, he didn't have to, he had Emma to guard him, so when the lady would drive down the long lane and get out of her car carrying a big cup of coffee, it was Emma who greeted her.

The lady would talk to her like you talk to a friend and pet Emma then say: "Let's go wake him up!" And they would dance to the house and run down the hall to the bedroom and jump on the bed.

The man would laugh and act surprised, but Emma knew better because he usually smelled like aftershave and toothpaste. That's not something you do for a smallish black lab.

Spring turned to summer and the days were rich with happiness. Then one bright September day, things changed. The man had not come home the night before. Sometimes he did that, but when he was going to be gone, he always left her extra food or made arrangements for one of the neighbors to come over and feed her. It's not that she was hungry, she just thought it was odd that he forgot her, and she showed her confusion by occasionally going to her bowl and looking at it. Where was he, where was The Man She Loved the Most?

It was Sunday and The Dancing Lady arrived earlier than usual but there was no coffee. Instead of hurrying into the house, she stood in the yard and stared at the bench under the tree for a long time.

Emma was happy to see her and frisked around the car expectantly. Maybe her man was with the lady. But the lady was alone and she very deliberately gave Emma an entire breakfast sandwich before walking to the house.

Emma was puzzled. She would run a few steps ahead of the lady then turn back and encourage her friend to dance, but there was no dancing. In the house, she would have dashed down the hall to the bedroom, only the lady stood in the dining room and shook her head.

Wanting very much to understand, the smallish dog came and sat at The Dancing Lady's feet. The lady talked to her and gently petted her as big salty drops of water fell on Emma's upturned face. She pressed into the lady's legs trying to comfort her and needing to be comforted in return because even though she was not very good with words, she truly understood emotions. And, somehow, Emma knew that The Man She Loved the Most was not coming back.

She sat by the lady until her friend moved away then went to the door and let herself out. It was morning and morning is the time you talk to God, so Emma trotted across the yard to the bench under the silver maple tree and jumped up on it. She laid down with her head on the spot where the man's lap would have been and, in her own way, talked to God.

The following days were hectic. A lot of people came and went, some she knew and some were strangers. Sometimes they fed her too much, sometimes too little, and sometimes not at all, but she didn't care.

When things quieted down, one of the man's daughters put the smallish dog and the bench from under the tree in her van and took them home with her. Emma liked the daughter and her family, and even though she missed her old friends, she was happy to be with people who cared about her and she wisely gave them all the love she had because that's what you do when you understand the way God loves. Emma was very smart that way.

To Emma who loved Jon the most:
Thank you for teaching me about God's love.
The Dancing Lady

Nothing

Her life amounted to nothing. She had accomplished nothing, gained nothing, and now, she felt nothing. Life had buffeted and disappointed Ruth to the point that, as she approached her forty-eighth birthday, she just didn't care anymore. The calluses that had grown between her expectations and her reality may have insulated her from pain, but they had also shut down her ability to feel. All she had left was an overwhelming sense of emptiness deepened by her upcoming class reunion.

Thirty years had passed since she graduated from high school. Thirty years! A lifetime! To Ruth, it seemed like many lifetimes, and nothing she had done had taken her life in the direction she wanted to go. In high school, Ruth had daydreamed of a successful career, wedded bliss, beautiful children, and *living happily ever after*. But all of her dreams had gone awry then dwindled down to nothing. There were no accomplishments, no awards, no rewards…

The Last Rose of Autumn

nothing of any value to account for all of those years. They were just gone.

Chilly night breezes teased at Ruth's hair pulling strands across her face, but the tickle did not penetrate her gloom and the dingy gray clouds that scudded across the sky and shrouded the moon did not catch her eye. Her attention focused on the black river flowing silently below. She knew that beneath the deceptively quiet surface, swift currents waited and would take her away just as relentlessly as the years had swept away her youth.

As Ruth stared into the flat black water, smothering waves of despair that grew from her emptiness inched her closer to the edge. Anything would have held her back, even anger would have given her something to hold onto, but Ruth had no anger. She had nothing, she felt nothing. Tired of it all, she released her hold on the rusty railing behind her, stepped out onto nothing, and silently dropped into the frigid water.

The shock of cold snatched away her breath and Ruth struggled to relax as she resisted her body's instinct to survive. The rushing current swept her along and she dispassionately watched the dim moonlight fading as the current pulled her lower and lower. Ruth felt totally removed from reality and the only thought hovering at the edge of her consciousness was that she hoped her life would not pass before her eyes. That would be too cruel.

Nothing

A soft glow in the water caught her attention. The image sharpened as it drew near and Ruth could see outstretched hands reaching for her. They gently began pulling her toward the surface. Her eyes followed the arms to find the person, and Ruth was surprised to see the face of an elderly woman she used to help at the grocery store. The lady had been dead for years and Ruth wondered if she was an angel sent by God to lead her home.

Ruth's assent stopped abruptly and she began to sink again. People who kill themselves don't go to heaven.

But before Ruth sank very far, other hands joined the old lady's and Ruth saw the faces of people long forgotten. There was the sickly little girl who lived next door when Ruth was a child. Ruth could not think of the little girl's name or what had made her ill, she just remembered sitting with her reading stories and playing quiet games until one day, her little friend had gone to the hospital and had not come back. The girl smiled at Ruth and she heard a hushed little voice speaking in her head: "You were my only friend."

Ruth strained to hear and other voices joined in: "You held the door for me." "You gave me $20 so my children could eat." "You taught me to read." "You answered phones at the telethon to raise money for my medical care." "I was old and alone and you listened to me." "I was grieving and you comforted me." "You saw me working and came to help." "I was lost and confused and you stopped your car so I could get through traffic."

Small things thought Ruth, such very small things which had cost her nothing could not amount to much.

"They were just nothing and I am nothing."

"Not to me," said a gentle voice that covered all the rest. The group around her receded and Ruth knew she was seeing the face of God. "You are *everything* to me."

Ruth heard the pain in His voice and knew she was breaking God's heart. The grief in His voice shattered the coldness in her heart and she threw out her hands to comfort Him.

"I'm so sorry!" she cried.

In that instant, her hands were caught in a firm grip and a surge in the current swirled and pushed her upward. The dizzying motion disoriented her and a grating firmness dragged against her shins and pitched her forward. When her hands hit the obstacle, Ruth realized she was on a sand bar.

Her lungs tore at her chest in a panic for air and she struggled toward the light above her stretching and thrashing in an effort to get her footing. As her head broke through the surface, she gasped and choked. Her wet clothes weighed her down, but the water was shallow and she staggered toward the shore coughing out the last of the river water.

When she got her bearings, she looked around to see if anyone was watching. Mercifully, no car lights

Nothing

lit the road or bridge, no voices called to see if she was okay. Remorse and embarrassment swept over Ruth and she hurried along the riverbank back to the bridge and her car.

Chills shook her and her teeth chattered uncontrollably, as much with delayed fear as with the cold. Water squished through the sides of her shoes and her wet coat slapped against her legs as she walked. She huddled her collar up around her neck to keep out the wind and raked her fingers through her hair as she self-consciously watched the road.

She keep looking around, but no one came to witness her folly and she found her car just as she had left it. The keys were in the ignition and the letter she had written lay on the front seat. For once, the uncooperative rattle trap started on the first try, and Ruth shrugged out of her soggy coat and wrapped up in the blanket she kept in the back seat. As she waited for the shaking to stop, she tore the letter into little shreds; then she drove home and spent the following weeks reevaluating her life as she tried to see it through eyes other than her own.

On the night of her class reunion, Ruth arrived wearing a flowered dress she had bought at a resale store. The style was out of date, but it looked very becoming on her and the bright colors banished any hint of dowdiness. Her hair was dyed a flattering, if unlikely shade of red, and her nails were painted a bold pink that matched her lipstick. She looked

The Last Rose of Autumn

lovely, but more than that, she had an inner glow that eclipsed all of her newfound outward beauty.

Ruth quietly had a good time and would never have believed that she was envied by many of her more worldly successful classmates. You see, Mouse, as they had nicknamed her in high school, had discovered something that continued to elude them:

She had discovered that the sandbars that save us are not made from boulders, they are formed by tiny acts of kindness and selflessness that accumulate below the surface where we don't notice them. And even though we build our own sandbars, it takes the love of God to pull us on to them.

A Funny Thing Happened Today

"*It was a dark and stormy night!*" Really, the wind blew for hours followed by lightning, thunder, and torrential rain. The electricity went out and the storm pounded on until just before sunrise when it finally let up. The peace that followed came like a welcome friend.

It seemed odd that what had sounded so fierce in the night could fade away so quickly, and I pondered that and other universal puzzles as I picked up sticks in the yard. I checked on the neighbors, and having done all I could do around the house, well all I chose to do, I decided to go for my usual morning walk.

When you live in the city and don't live near a park, it's a challenge to find pleasant places to walk, so I felt fortunate to have found a large quiet area generously dotted with trees and crisscrossed with paved drives. The fact that it was a cemetery may

The Last Rose of Autumn

put off some people, but I felt very comfortable there. It was a great place to stretch my legs, and I knew from having grown up in a small town with a big cemetery that visitors discourage vandals.

I passed the main gate and went in on the South entering through "The Baby Gate". I called it that because the first section you come to is row on row of small headstones marking the graves of infants. From time to time, someone would place flowers on one of the little graves, but most of them were so old that the parents had to be gone too. My heart went out to these babies laid to rest away from their families. I don't suppose that matters to you when you're dead, but I felt sorry for them anyway and would always pray that these little ones and the people who had loved them would all have peace.

As I turned the loop at the farthest point from the gate and headed back, I saw an old man tugging at a large limb that had fallen over a headstone and went to help him. He was old and frail, and I prayed for him too.

He came often and would take a folding lawn chair from the trunk of his car and carry it to a grave that always had a modest little handful of flowers propped by it. He would set up his chair, check the flowers, dust the stone with his handkerchief, then sit down and read out loud from a little notebook he carried in his shirt pocket.

I'm the curious sort, so one day when he was not there, I had walked across the grass to see what was

A Funny Thing Happened Today

carved on the stone. On one half was a lady's name followed by "Beloved Wife and Mother". She would have been about his age and since the other half of the stone was a man's name with a birth date only, I assumed she was his wife and that he missed her.

The limb he was trying to wrestle looked to be mostly leaves and I probably could have moved it by myself; however, my mother did not raise an idiot. I knew better than to tell him to step aside and do it myself. Okay, I have done some really stupid things in my life, but I *was* listening when she told me it's unkind to make old men feel useless; so I took hold of the limb in the middle allowing me carry most of the weight and more or less followed his directions as we dragged the limb to the side of the drive.

We walked back to see if the stone was damaged and again my curiosity got the better of me. When he thanked me, I remarked that I had frequently seen him. What I did not say was that I hoped he would tell me what he was reading. Obligingly enough, he did anyway.

"I do come here a lot when the weather's nice," he replied. "I'm sorry I didn't notice you, I sort of get wrapped up in what I'm doing. This is my dear wife and I like to come and read to her. You see, I went to war right after we got married and the mail was slow and unreliable back then, so I took to writing down funny things that would happen thinking that when I got back home, I'd share them with my Anna. But

The Last Rose of Autumn

when I got back, there was so much new stuff to talk about, I never got around to it.

"Then I went to work at the GM factory and every time something would tickle my funny bone, I'd write it down. By then, we had kids and my mom lived with us, Anna sure had her hands full. When I got home at night, she just needed for me to listen, so that's what I did. She always had a lot to tell me and I loved to hear her talk. Something funny that happened at work didn't seem anywhere near as important as a new tooth or first step; so I put my thoughts on the back burner and kept on writing things down in these little notebooks. It didn't matter anyway, I figured there would be plenty of time later.

"Before you know it, the kids were grown, Mom was gone, and I'd retired. Anna and I traveled and acted like a couple of silly kids. We had a lot of fun. Then Anna got sick and even though she was quiet most of the time, I was not about to waste one precious minute talking when I might still hear her lovely voice. How could dusty old stories compare to that?

"Then she was gone. At first, there was so much to do that I was busy all the time; but when things settled down, I got lonely. One day, I was cleaning a closet and found a couple of shoe boxes full of notebooks and decided to bring them when I came over here and share them with her. I don't suppose anybody will care about my memories when I'm gone, but they've lightened my days," he said pulling a

A Funny Thing Happened Today

dog-eared little notebook out of his shirt pocket and smoothing out the corners. "I'm up to 1952."

"That's the year I was born," I told him as my good angel nudged me. I unfolded his lawn chair and placed it in a level spot then seated myself on a neighboring headstone and asked him if he would like to read some of his notes to me. After asking me if I was sure, he joyfully flipped through the pages and began to read. With a few explanations of names and relationships, I quickly became acquainted with his coworkers and friends, and truly enjoyed his memories. He was a good story-teller with a droll sense of humor and a lively appreciation for the ridiculous. It was easy to see he had lived a cup-half-full kind of life.

When he grew tired, I warmly thanked him and helped him back to his car. As I walked home, I thought about Anna and envied and pitied her at the same time. I thought she was very blessed to have had a husband who loved her so much that he had selflessly put aside his own day-to-day thoughts so he could support her. And I also felt more than a little sorry for her because she had missed out on an aspect of his life I think she would have enjoyed very much.

That was a long time ago, but I still think of Anna and her hero and pray that somewhere in Heaven there are two comfy lawn chairs sitting side-by-side in the shade, and that she is finally getting to hear the funny things that happened while he was busy loving her.

"Greater love has no one than this, than to lay down one's life for his friends."

Birdhouses

"Shellie, honey, have you signed up yet? There are still several seats available on the bus for the shopping trip to the mall and you know we'll have a good time," promised Mrs. Collins.

Shellie looked forlorn as she set a can of green beans in her grocery cart. "I can't go. Ben will be out of town next week and there isn't any way Dad can stay by himself."

"Oh sweetie, I'm so sorry, I didn't think about that. I wonder if there's somebody who could help? What about Mrs. Tredway, she's a retired nurse, maybe she would stay with him."

"She does sometimes, but her daughter is pregnant and on bed rest. Mrs. Tredway went to take care of the other children. There are three of them, you know."

"Gosh, I didn't know that. She's such a nice lady, I sure hope things turn out well for her daughter, but I still hate it that you can't go to the mall with us.

You spend so much time taking care of Gus, I'd love to see you get out for a day to do your Christmas shopping and just have some fun," she added warmly patting Shellie's arm.

A deep voice spoke her name and Shellie turned around. Leighton, the man who had been her father's best friend stood behind her. The two men had been closer than brothers until something had broken them apart and strained the relationship between the two families. Shellie had no idea what had caused the split. She could not discover that harsh words had been spoken or insults traded, they had simply stopped talking. And now with her mother and brother gone and her father suffering from Alzheimer's, she longed for her old friends more than ever.

"Hello!" she eagerly greeted him then abruptly paused not knowing what to do next.

Once upon a time, she would have been certain of a big hug, now she didn't know if he would even shake her hand. Mercifully, there were too many grocery carts between them to make her discomfort obvious. Mrs. Collins knew there were issues and tactfully excused herself thinking they might do better without a third party.

"How's Max?" asked Shellie groping for conversation by referring to Leighton's younger son, the one closest in age to herself.

"Max is fine, he finishes his residency in two months. Rather frightening isn't it, the kid who

Birdhouses

used to pull the heads off your dolls becoming a pediatrician?"

Shellie laughed, but the young woman looked thin and the dark circles under her eyes concerned Leighton. She and her husband had sold their home in the city and moved in with Shellie's dad to take care of him. The relocation required her husband, Ben, to be away from home several times a month leaving the full burden of caring for Gus and their four-year-old daughter, Lily, on Shellie. It was a lot to handle and Leighton wondered if she was losing ground as the Alzheimer's that muddled Gus's mind progressed.

Of the four children he and Gus had fathered, Shellie was the only girl and Leighton would always regard her in a special way. Standing here looking in her tired eyes, his heart melted. "Shell, I want you to go on this shopping trip with the ladies. I'll spend the day with Gus."

Overcome, she blinked back tears that stung her eyelids and forlornly shook her head. "You don't know what you'd be getting into," she murmured. "Daddy doesn't know who people are anymore. He thinks I'm Lily, and most days...most days he doesn't even know his own name. He's not mean or hard to get along with, he just talks about the past a lot and stares off into space; but you have to watch him every minute—remind him to eat and drink, go to the bathroom, not to wander off, And sometimes, when his memory comes back for a few minutes, he becomes very agitated. It freaks him out to be hop-scotching through time with no control over it. He doesn't understand what's happening..." and her voice broke.

More than ever convinced she needed help, Leighton pushed the grocery carts aside and took her shoulders pulling her into a warm embrace. Her arms curled against her chest as she rested her head on his heart and soaked in the comfort. She took several short breaths fighting back the tears that threatened to overwhelm her and, for a few minutes, allowed her burdens to drift away as her mind went back in time to a happier place.

Before Shellie was ready, a loud crash of falling cans in the next aisle jolted her back to reality and she pressed her face into Leighton's shirt taking one last whiff of him.

"It's too much to ask," she said flatly.

He gave her his fatherly—my mind is made up so don't argue—look and replied: "We'll be okay, we'll make birdhouses." She looked doubtful. "I'll get all of the cutting done ahead of time and we'll just assemble them. He'll like that and we won't use anything more dangerous than a tack hammer."

Shellie knew Leighton was right about Gus enjoying the process of building birdhouses, he had loved working with wood. He and Leighton used to spend hours in each other's workshops and she remembered her dad saying: "There's something about the smell of sawdust that's restful to the soul."

Birdhouses

"Are you sure?" she hedged.

"We'll be fine. Sally Perkins and some of the ladies from church are hosting a day out for kids, Lily can go there and Gus will come with me. Send me an email with instructions."

So plans were made and Leighton arrived at the house a few minutes before 7:00 on the appointed day. He felt odd standing on Gus's front porch, it had been a long time. Through the front window, he saw Miss Lily hopping down the stairs with one shoe on and one shoe in her hand while Shellie tucked the things her daughter would need for the day into a pink back pack.

"Put your shoe on, cupcake!" called Shellie. "Oh, come in Leighton. Lily, do you remember Mr. Leighton?" Lily nodded and bashfully held her shoe in front of her face and peeked under it.

"Sit down, Cinderella, and I'll help you with your glass slipper," he offered.

"It's not a glass slipper," she informed him with a goofy grin as she obediently plopped down on the bottom step allowing this fun person to help her with the shoelaces that were knotted.

As he worked on the laces, Leighton casually glanced around and saw the back of Gus's head. He was sitting in his favorite chair watching television seemingly unaware that a visitor was a few feet away. Lily's knight kept up a stream of jovial conversation to hide his nervousness, but the butterflies in his stomach were going crazy.

When he finished, Shellie went to Gus and told him Leighton was there to spend the day with him. She helped her dad bring the recliner to its upright position so he could stand up, and the man Leighton had not spoken to in years turned to face him.

Gus had gotten very old in the years they had been apart. His graying hair looked grizzled and needed cut, but he was cleanly shaved and had on a nice plaid shirt and a cardigan sweater. And even though the sweater was miss-buttoned and his socks didn't match, he looked fresh and ready for a day out.

Shellie spoke brightly as she talked to him: "This is Leighton, you're going to spend the day with him while we have a girl's day out."

Gus inclined his head toward his daughter politely listening the way you would listen to a stranger then immediately extended his hand to Leighton. "Very nice to make your acquaintance, Leighton. Are you new here?"

Thrown for a moment, Leighton blinked then made a fast recovery and shook his old friend's hand replying: "I've been here a while, but I'm hoping you can fill me in on some of the local history."

"Glad to!" responded Gus pleased to have made a new friend.

The girls were ready to go and Gus pulled out his wallet and slipped Lily a couple of dollars whispering that she might need some money. Leighton caught the flicker of pain in Shellie's eyes as her dad kissed

Birdhouses

his granddaughter goodbye and treated his daughter as if she were some nice person he did not know.

Stepping into the gap, Leighton put his arm around Shellie's shoulders and pressed a folded stack of bills into her hand as he planted a kiss on top of her head and advised her to shake a leg. She tried to protest, but he refused to take back the money apologetically saying: "I've missed way too many of your birthdays," and her heartache was eased by the return of his love.

The men went to have breakfast at a local cafe and joined a group of seniors seated around a large oval table in what was good-naturedly referred to as The Geezer Corner. Several of the men greeted Gus and he responded congenially. Watching him, Leighton realized you had to listen carefully or you would not notice that Gus was bluffing his way through the conversation. He was warm and friendly asking lots of questions and listening earnestly, but he never called anyone by name unless someone else had just done so and his obscure answers about current events would have made a seasoned politician proud.

Leighton sat silently observing, he had always been the more reticent of the two and no one seemed to notice he had little to say.

A mutual friend took a chair next to Leighton and quietly commented: "I'm glad to see you guys together again. It wasn't the same without you, and I think it'll do Gus good."

The Last Rose of Autumn

"I'm not sure what will help Gus," replied Leighton a sadly. "But it *will* do Shellie good, so I'm glad I can help."

The general conversation flowed easily and everything was fine until a loud, tactless man asked a question about a restaurant Gus and his wife used to frequent. Leighton knew Gus should have been able to answer the question and cringed inwardly when he was at a loss.

"No, I don't recall ever having been there," responded Gus with a confused look on his face. The man was shocked and blusteringly insisted Gus knew the place. The confused look turned into a troubled expression and Gus began to twitch and nervously shake his head.

Leighton intervened saying that Gus had been ill and that his memory was not as sharp as it used to be. The quelling look he gave the loud man silenced him, but Gus continued to be bothered as he struggled to find the information misplaced in his mind. A few minutes later, Leighton announced it was time for them to visit the barber and the two left.

After they got their hair cut, they went to the grain elevator to buy birdseed and stopped at the post office to get some stamps. Then they went by the bank where Leighton used to be president so he could get the papers he needed to review before the next board meeting. At every stop, Gus was talkative and gregarious but the nervous twitch did not leave; and when their conversation lapsed into

Birdhouses

silence, Leighton could see that his companion was still wrestling with confusion.

Leighton's wife was on the shopping trip with the other women and had left lunch for the guys in a crock pot. They shared a pleasant meal then went to the basement. Gus had been an easy guest to entertain and had readily gone along with all of the day's plans, so Leighton was not surprised when he had agreed to the suggestion that they might enjoy a little carpentry. What did surprise him was the change that came over Gus as he walked down the stairs to the work shop

The kitchen where he had eaten hundreds of meals and drank thousands of cups of coffee had left no impression, the workshop was different and made him pause and look around. He breathed in the smell of it and said, "Boy-o-boy, sawdust sure is good for the soul!" And the twitch left him.

They started to assemble the birdhouses Leighton had prepared, and before long, Gus pulled forward a tall stool and took his wallet out of his hip pocket putting it on the workbench before he sat down. It was the same stool he had always chosen and his wallet rested in what he had called *his* spot. Observing this, Leighton knew that somewhere inside his jumbled thoughts, the old Gus was still there.

As they worked, Gus caught Leighton unawares when he said: "I used to build little things like this with a friend of mine. Best guy I ever knew in my life. Best friend a man could have."

Hating himself but desperately needing to understand, Leighton asked: "Still spend time with him?"

"No," answered Gus shaking his head regretfully; "we had a falling out and I haven't seen him in a long time. I sure miss him though."

"What happened?"

"I'm not sure I should say," he began, "but I don't suppose it matters now. Most of the people concerned are dead so the truth won't hurt them. My son was different, wild and mixed up, always ready to try any crazy adventure that came along. Well, he tried the wrong things and got sick, that sickness you get from promiscuous sex and illegal drugs. I can't remember what you call it, but you don't get over it. Hell, they didn't even have a name for it back then, so we put him in a clinic that treated cases like his and prayed.

"The father of one of his roommates turned out to be the owner of a successful company that was expanding into our area. Good sort of fella and a shrewd business-man. Well, he was shopping for a local bank and had decided to use my friend's bank; *that* would have been a wise decision. When he found out I ran a bank too, he changed his mind and approached us. I didn't want his business. It was too much personal stress besides not being the kind of transactions we were set up to handle, but he insisted. The board found out, and I didn't have a choice.

"It was awful. To make matters worse, it wasn't my secret and I couldn't tell my best friend why the

Birdhouses

man had changed his mind, and I was too ashamed to admit what was wrong with my boy. I was such a fool. I let fear and pride cheat me out of the best friend a man could have on this side of Heaven."

He paused and turned haunted eyes to Leighton. "Do you think if he knew the truth...do you think a man could forgive his friend for being such a fool?"

"If he was my friend, I would," answered Leighton honestly.

Gus went quiet for a few minutes then suddenly exclaimed: "Wow! Smells like somebody messed their pants."

Leighton gasped. He had gotten so comfortable with Gus that he had forgotten to remind him to go to the bathroom. The look on his host's face told Gus too much and he stood up cautiously feeling the back of his pants.

"*It's me,*" he whispered appalled and embarrassed. "It's me! Oh my God, it's me!" he cried shaking his head futilely trying to deny the truth. His eyes met Leighton's in horrified desperation, then the look on Gus's face changed.

"Leighton? Leighton, what happened to you? You're an old man. What happened to me?" he demanded in a panicked voice as he stared at the back of his own wrinkled hands and tried to rub away the liver spots. "What the hell is going on? I feel like I'm in the Twilight Zone! Am I crazy? Where am I? How'd I get here!"

The Last Rose of Autumn

Leighton forced himself to speak calmly: "You're not crazy," he reassured Gus. "Well, no crazier than you ever were," he added with the license of an old friend trying to lighten the situation. "You have Alzheimer's and you forget things. You're at my house. You're safe. You're with me."

The evenness of his voice had a calming effect on Gus and he reached out to grasp Leighton's arm as if it were a lifeline that would link him to something that made sense. "You brought me here, so we're all right."

It was more of a question than a statement and Leighton answered from the depths of his soul: "Yes, we're all right."

"Maggie?" asked Gus referring to his wife.

"Gone. Laid down to take a nap and just didn't wake up." Gus nodded prosaically accepting the death of his wife as something that was probably for the best.

"My boy, Jay, is he gone too?" Leighton nodded and Gus nodded again, "And what about my baby, my little Shellie? Is she alright?" he asked poignantly.

Pleased to be able to give his friend some good news, Leighton smiled. "Oh, she's terrific, Gus. All grown up and married to a fine young man. You walked her down the aisle and she was so proud of you. They have a beautiful daughter who's a little character, she's just like Shellie. Here, you have a picture of them in your wallet," and he opened Gus's

Birdhouses

wallet to show him the picture he carried of Shellie and her family.

The picture was not new, but he looked at it as if seeing it for the first time. It could have been the picture that came in the wallet for all he knew. He ran his hand over it trying to make some connection to the pretty young woman he did not recognize and began to sob. "My baby, my precious little girl all grown up, and I don't remember. I don't know who she is."

As his face crumpled, Leighton locked his arms around his best friend and they cried together.

Several minutes later, Leighton reached into a cabinet to get paper towels they could use as hand-kerchiefs and he saw his old Bible on the shelf. It was the first Bible he had owned, and he and Gus had had many edifying debates over its messages. They had challenged themselves, kept each other on track, and grown as believers through reading it. The people at their church had called them "David and Jonathan" and the two had good naturedly tussled over who was who. Leighton put the Bible away the day he heard about the bank deal, now he knew it was long past time to bring it out again.

He handed Gus a wad of paper towels and laid the Bible on the workbench. Gus wiped his eyes and blew his nose then looked down at the Bible. He stroked the cover and smiled. "I really like this book. I don't recall the name of it, but I sure do like it."

The Last Rose of Autumn

Something in the tone of his voice informed Leighton that his friend had slipped into the fog again, and although he was grieved, he felt at peace. In spite of the circumstances, he had his best friend back and that counted for a lot.

"Come on, buddy, let's get you cleaned up."

"Okay, buddy," said Gus reaching out to take his hand with the trust of a small child.

They had been more than friends. They had been David and Jonathan, iron sharpening iron, deep calling to deep, armor bearers for each other. But there were other bearers in the Bible, and sometimes you have to chop a hole in the roof and hold on tight trusting Jesus to do the rest.

A Shirt for Joe

"*Mercy!*" she exclaimed. There was so much to do before the kids got there and she didn't know what to do first.

"*I can do all things through Christ who strengthens me!*" she affirmed and started to wipe her hands on her apron. She grimaced and spread out the faded cotton fabric feeling hopelessly outdated. Nobody wears aprons anymore! But she had gotten into the habit as a girl and it just seemed natural.

"Oh well, I never set out to be a fashion model," she sighed heading into the bedroom to organize her husband's clothes. His suit was fine, but Joe would need a nice white shirt; hmmm, he had worn his best one two nights ago and it was still in the dirty clothesbasket.

Sorting through the crumpled clothes, she quickly found the shirt and held it up by the collar. Drat! It had a speck of spaghetti sauce on the front, so she headed to the kitchen to rub the little dab of dish soap into it. As she went, she sang:

Leaning, leaning, safe and secure from all alarms.
Leaning, leaning, I'm leaning on the
everlasting arms.

Reaching for the dish soap, she realized that she could wash this one item out in the sink faster than she could do a whole load of clothes and quickly ran some water. She scrubbed out the spot, briskly rubbed the collar between her hands, and rinsed the shirt twice to get all of the soap out. Then she put the shirt on a plastic hanger and hung it from the flower basket hook on the summer kitchen porch. It would be dry in no time.

Wiping her hands on her apron again, she looked out across the wide yard and over the fence to the lush green pasture that was dotted with white cows. She saw the big red barn they had painted last year and the machinery shed that needed painting this year. Parked next to the shed was a little gray Ford tractor, the first piece of brand new machinery they had purchased. They had been so proud of that little tractor.

From there, her gaze ran along the hedge fence posts that lined the gravel driveway, then she looked across the oiled road studying the wheat field that stretched on the other side. The long stalks swirled and swayed with the wind, their heads bowed down full of grain. That field would be ready to harvest soon, but right now, it looked like an ocean of gold.

She turned and her eyes followed the line of the oiled road until her view was blocked by the walnut trees growing in the yard beside the house. The leaves were so thick that the grass looked black in their dense shade. Those trees had been skinny saplings when she and Joe first moved here. It seemed like yesterday.

Her mind drifted back over the years and she smiled at the memories as she stood with her arm wrapped around the white porch post like it was an old friend she was standing arm-in-arm with. The wind blew softly and she lifted her face to the warm afternoon sun and stared at the clouds silently floating over head. It seemed wasteful. Wonderful and always different, they were there every day for her enjoyment, but she seldom thought to look up other than to check the weather. She breathed in deeply trying to take in and hold a little bit of the serenity around her.

"I don't say *thank you* enough, Lord. You have given me a precious and beautiful place to live and I really am grateful. Thank you!" and as she went back to her chores, she hummed:

This is my Father's world, He shines in all that's fair; in the rustling grass I hear Him pass, He speaks to me Everywhere...

Half an hour later, she stepped back onto the porch to check the shirt. It was just right, so she took it down and carried it into the summer kitchen where she kept her ironing board set up. The iron was hot in no time and she set to work spritzing the shirt with spray starch and pressing crisp creases into the soft cotton fabric. As she ironed, she recalled some of the times her husband had worn this shirt. The first time had been for their 50th wedding anniversary, then their granddaughter had gotten married, great-grandchildren had gotten baptized, life had been pleasant.

Reminiscing made time pass too quickly and the closer she got to being finished, the slower her hands moved as if finishing the task would be the end of something she did not want to let go of. She hesitated then stopped trying to avoid the inevitable and slipped the shirt back on the hanger and reached up to hook it on the door. As she did, she caught the soft scent of Joe's aftershave that lingered in the fabric and pressed her hands to her mouth as she burst into tears.

Blindly reaching for a battered wooden chair, she sank down on to it and let go of the tears that had gathered in her heart for fifty-three years. For fifty-three years she had been happy and had had very little use for tears. Now, all of those unused tears spilled down her face and she rocked back and forth trying to ease the unbearable sadness that gripped her. Her grief overflowed and she beat her fist against her lap and jammed wadded handfuls of apron against her mouth wailing inconsolably.

After a while, the tears slowed but she clung to the arm of the chair and continued to rock. "Life's not fair," she whispered. "I know that. No one promised me it would be." All things considered though, she knew it had been more fair to her than to many others, and she fished in her apron pocket for a tissue.

She stood up and went to the shirt running her hands along the sleeves that had held her so many times. Lovingly wrapping them around her shoulders, she gently rested her head against the shirt front...just for a moment...just once more.

She felt the warmth of the late afternoon sun as it shone through the screen door, and a breeze stirred the shirt. One of the sleeves fluttered in the ghost of a pat and a damp smile trembled on her lips. Ready to go on, she dried her eyes on her apron and brokenly sang:

I come to the garden alone
While the dew is still on the roses
And the voice I hear falling on my ear
The Son of God discloses.
And He walks with me, and He talks with me,
And He tells me I am His own...

Escape from Gomorrah

"*A*re you sure he wants to see *me*? He doesn't like me, at all, and I'm not his daughter-in-law anymore. Matthew and I got divorced three years ago. If The Reverend has been ill, he might be having hallucinations; you should call his wife, Mrs. *Jane* Sanderson."

Lacey could not think of a more likely explanation for this unusual turn of events. Rigid and conservative, The Reverend had done everything possible to keep his son away from her before they were married; and in spite of his vehement stand against divorce, he had been openly relieved when they had parted. Colorful and spirit-filled, Lacey had been way too much for him to swallow back then, why would he want to see her now?

The nurse assured Lacey that her former father-in-law *was* in his right mind and asking to see her. "He said you may not want to come, but he requests that you do."

Escape from Gomorrah

The Reverend's requests had always sounded a lot like orders to Lacey and she was torn. The nurse waited patiently while she wrestled with her better self and old wounds until she finally sighed: "All right, when?"

"Could you come at 1:00 this afternoon?" Lacey agreed and made arrangements to leave work early.

Later, it occurred to her that Matthew had recently sold his dot com business. Perhaps The Reverend thought she would go after his son's money and wanted to remind her how unworthy he judged her to be. This was a message she had heard many times and it irked her to be rearranging her day to visit someone who had made her life miserable while confidently believing he was nothing less than the divine voice of God, but she would go. He was old and sick and she was a nicer person than he was. She would grumble to herself all the way there and probably all the way back, but she would go.

Driving to the hospital, Lacey thought about her ex-husband and how they had started this journey. Matthew had approached her at a college dance. Not interested, she had been dauntingly repellent coldly telling the serious-looking grad student that buttoned-down oxford cloth was not her style. He had taken her rejection good-naturedly and moved away from her group to stand by the wall with some other guys.

Quietly confident, he certainly had not looked like a kicked puppy, but when her friends made him the butt of several crude jokes, Lacey had stopped them and motioned him to the dance floor with an ungracious jerk of her head. His answering smile had been just humble enough to appease her, and his old school manners charmed her as he politely moved a chair out of her way and stepped aside for her to go ahead of him.

The band had been playing fast songs but transitioned into a slow love song as the mismatched couple reached the dance floor. Lacey had hesitated. A slow, close dance was not what she had mentally bargained for, but she was not one to back down and had responded to the light pressure of his hand on the small of her back and moved to a less crowded area of the floor.

Matthew was a good dancer and the subtle scent of his after-shave reminded her of limes. Fighting against the tide, Lacey had looked him in the eye and bluntly demanded: "Why me?"

"I think you're beautiful and smart," he had replied with a smile that made her pulse flutter.

"Anyone can see that I'm beautiful," she had countered sparring for time. "Why do you think I'm smart?"

"I heard you present your paper in Dr. Shepherd's class. You made several interesting points."

That had surprised a laugh out of her. If he understood her paper, he was no mental lightweight and she did grudgingly find him attractive; so they danced again...and again, then he had walked her

Escape from Gomorrah

back to her dorm. He was an untimely distraction, she didn't want a boyfriend, but he kept asking and she kept saying yes. Then he had taken her to meet his parents.

Mrs. Jane Sanderson had been stunned by her son's interesting new friend but willing to get to know Lacey before forming an opinion. The Reverend, fifteen years older than his lovely wife and unbending in his ways, was not so generous and had not been able to see past Lacey's multi-colored hair and avant-garde clothes. When he asked what classes she was taking, his condescending tone annoyed Lacey and she had vaguely replied: a class to help her write papers, some math, chemistry, sociology, and the Science of Color.

Humph! Fashion Merchandising assumed The Reverend; and once he had made up his mind, it had not been altered by the fact that Lacey was a chemistry honors student with a full scholarship and a great job offer from a large paint manufacturer. He loudly disapproved of what he believed to be his son's infatuation with this unconventional young woman and told them they were too young to be spending so much time together. Harshly critical of the couple, he had ordered them to end the relationship at once.

Biting back angry words, Matthew had apologized to his mother telling her that he and Lacey would go out for pizza instead of dining with the family. Four months later, he and Lacey had gotten

The Last Rose of Autumn

married by a justice of the peace. The Reverend had gone nuclear.

"Blessed are the peacemakers..." and poor Jane had negotiated numerous armed truces even though peace rarely lasted long. The Reverend wanted his son to follow in his footsteps and envisioned Matthew taking over his church. Matthew saw himself head of his own successful company. And Lacey had just wanted to see more of her workaholic husband. The end came for her when Matthew forgot their fifth anniversary and went to spend the evening with his father. The Reverend had not forgotten the significance of the day and had deliberately made plans that excluded Lacey. Fed up with being last in her husband's life and tired of seeing him pulled to pieces, Lacey left.

Years had passed, but the wounds were still raw. She dreaded having to meet The Reverend again and stalled by stopping to pick up a small gift. Unable to find a card that expressed her true sentiments and recalling that her ex-father-in-law considered flowers a waste of money, she walked around the store agonizing and finally purchased a box of Puffs. If you looked at it in light of what hospitals charge for a small box of coarse, half-size tissues, it was a very thoughtful gift.

She arrived a few minutes early and waited in the hall until the second hand was swinging up to the twelve before going into his room. The Reverend had frequently lectured her about punctuality and

Escape from Gomorrah

she was not willing to hand him another opportunity to display his look of resigned disappointment. She was ready for a fight, but everything changed as she walked into the room and saw how the once powerfully built man had declined. She paused. He looked so old and drawn that her animosity melted and her heart went out to him. When he turned his head toward her and held out his hand in welcome, she immediately set her things down and took his hand in both of hers.

"Lacey! I'm so grateful you came."

Mindful of the many bruises and puncture marks on his thin skin, she would have released him but his clasp did not loosen. Unwilling to rebuff him, she gingerly sat down on the side of the bed and they talked about the weather and general news for several minutes until he emotionally said: "I never got the chance to thank you in person for bringing Ariadne back to us."

Lacey tried to make light of her actions but he would not allow it. As he poured out his heart, Lacey recalled the events from two years ago.

Twelve years younger than Matthew, his kid sister Ariadne had been a handful. Her name might mean "most holy" but it did not describe The Reverend's daughter; about a year after the divorce, the rebellious teenager had thrown off the shackles of being a pastor's child and run away.

Confident that his erring child was safe and would come home in a few days, her father had done

The Last Rose of Autumn

nothing. That was a mistake. The days had turned into weeks and the weeks into months and still there was no sign of Ariadne or word of her whereabouts. Assuming she was a runaway, the police had refused to do more than add her name to a list of missing persons, and two private detectives hired by the Sandersons had searched in vain.

Hesitant to come under fire for interfering, Lacey had waited until she heard that the second private detective failed. After that, she began to search on her own going out nearly every night to walk the streets checking out soup kitchens, homeless shelters, and crash pads, any place runaways hung out.

After two months of chasing false leads and wearing herself out, Lacey had felt discouraged but would not give up. Still angry about her marriage, she had not spoken to God for quite a while; then late one night as she walked to her car preparing to search again, she had earnestly cried out to God: "Lord, I've got to find her!"

"Then why don't you ask me where she is?" He had replied. Aghast that she might be throwing Ariadne to the wolves by selfishly being angry with God, Lacey had apologized at once and begged for direction. He spoke to her again asking: "Do you trust me?"

"Yes," she answered without reservation. Immediately she had a vision of rundown apartments over an abandoned storefront and somehow knew that the building was in a town forty miles away. The question was: in what part of the town? *"Please*, Father, show me how to get there," and she had started her car and headed for the highway.

En route, she had to pass a deli that Ariadne liked and heard God say: "Get some soup." So she stopped to pick up a large insulated container of Ariadne's favorite.

For the next hour, she had followed God's directions: take this exit, veer left, turn at the light, and eventually had found herself parked a block away from the building she had seen in the vision.

Getting her bearings, Lacey muttered: "There was an easier way to get here, you know."

"I know," confirmed God, "you needed some practice following directions. What's coming will not be easy."

She had been away from God for a long time and fear tried to overcome her. Unwilling to surrender, she had strengthened herself in the Lord thanking Him for His faithfulness and grace, and she pushed the attack aside. Lacey knew that if she just trusted God, everything would work out.

"...all things work together for the good of those who love God, to those who are called according to His purpose." She had whispered over and over followed by: *"I know that You can do everything and that no purpose of Yours can be withheld from You."*

"In Jesus name, please Father, let it be Your purpose that Ariadne is okay and that she comes back with me and gets her life straightened out," she prayed and great peace surrounded her as she had walked past the rough-looking people loitering near the building and calmly climbed the stairs.

As she walked, verses from Psalm 91 kept circling in her head,

For He shall give His angels charge over you, to keep you in all your ways. In their hands they shall bear you up, lest you dash your foot against a stone. You shall tread upon the lion and the cobra, the young lion and the serpent you shall trample underfoot.

At the top of the stairs, Lacey opened the main door and gagged at the stench. The odor of dirty bodies mixed with rotting garbage, poor sanitation, and burning drugs challenged her resolve and she had prayed harder as she went from room to room looking for the girl who had been a little sister to her. In the dim light, she would have walked past a disheveled figure lying on a broken down sofa but the Lord stopped her and Lacey shook the person's arm.

"Go away!" whined a slurred voice, and Lacey recognized her sister-in-law.

Heavy-hearted and grossed out by the girl's condition, Lacey wanted to cry. Instead she forced herself to sound cheerful and shook Ariadne again. "Hey, sleepy-head. It's Lacey. Get up!"

"Lacey? Awh, I love Lacey, but she wouldn' be here. This's a awful place and you're jus a dream. *Go away!*" she commanded even though her voice broke.

Escape from Gomorrah

Undeterred, Lacey persisted and had gotten the stoned Ariadne to struggle to her feet by promising soup.

To keep the girl from falling down, Lacey pulled Ariadne's arm across her shoulders and they were heading to the stairs when a menacing figure had blocked the hallway.

"Where the hell do you think you're taking her?" he had demanded in a voice that sent chills down Lacey's back and caused Ariadne to quiver.

Lacey wanted to shriek for him to get out of her way before she called the cops but the Lord had bound her tongue and Ariadne had stammered in a placating voice: "We...we jus gonna have some soop. Iss okay. Iss jus soop. Okay?"

Lacey hated the man for the cowering way Ariadne was acting and blamed him for what had happened to the girl.

He sneered. Apparently, going out for soup was not okay with him and he moved forward reaching to take Ariadne away from Lacey. His hand was inches from her when he had abruptly stopped as if an unseen force barred his way and he recoiled as his dark gaze focused on something behind the women. Repelled, he had backed away into the darkness, leaving without an explanation.

Intensely curious but unafraid of what he had seen, Lacey half dragged, half carried Ariadne down the stairs and out of the building firmly repeating: "Don't look back, Ari, *don't look back!*"

The Last Rose of Autumn

Relieved that her car with all of its tires was where she had left it, Lacey had wrangled Ariadne into the passenger seat and distracted her with the container of soup. While the girl ate, Lacey put as much distance as she could between them and the horrible building. The soup helped Ariadne sober up, but with reality came fear, and she kept asking Lacey to take her back because *he* would be angry. Since the only "he" Lacey feared was the He who had created the heavens and the earth, she had kept on driving and gently reminded Ariadne that the girl had given her life to a higher power and that relationship was more important than anything.

Before long, her passenger fell asleep and they had continued on through the night to the Sanderson's home.

A few blocks from the house, a police siren had startled Ariadne and she awoke with a jerk. Recognizing where she was, she again begged Lacey to take her back. Still unwilling to give up, Lacey had asked Ariadne to just go look at her parent's house; then if she still wanted to leave, they would. Ariadne moaned and rocked back and forth but had agreed reasoning that the sooner she looked, the sooner they could leave.

As they neared the house, Lacey switched off the car lights and parked. Notoriously frugal, The Reverend had always insisted that all unnecessary lights should be turned off; but even though it was nearing 3:30 in the morning, the porch lights blazed and a lamp glowed in the front window. The light from the lamp seemed to change colors and Ariadne stared in disbelief as she struggled to focus.

"That's my ballerina lamp! Sometimes Daddy would let me keep it on at night when I was afraid," she mused in a little-girl voice.

"He's the one who's afraid now," explained Lacey. "He won't allow anyone to turn off the lights because he's afraid you'll come home and find the house dark and think they don't care. Oh sweetie, they love you so much! He and your mom take turns staying up all night praying for you, and one of them is always here. They won't even go to church together because you might come by and they would miss you."

Ariadne's moans turned into muffled sobs. "Lace, I wanna go home...*I wanna go home!*"

"Let's go!" replied her rescuer starting to get out of the car.

"No! I can't," breathed Ariadne in a panicked voice as she grabbed Lacey's arm pulling her back. "You don't know what I've done. You don't know. Daddy'll be so mad at me," she whispered tearfully. "He'll yell!"

A gurgle of irrepressible laughter escaped Lacey and she had brushed the tangled hair back from Ariadne's face and gently forced her to look up. "Duh!"

Accepting this simple truth, Ariadne laughed too then wiped her eyes on her cuff as she fumbled for the door handle.

Lacey had walked her to the front steps then put Ariadne's hand on the rail and turned to walk away.

"Don't leave me!"

"You have to go the rest of the way by yourself, babe. It's like that walk down to the front when you get saved. It's something only you can do. I won't leave until I know you're okay."

Ariadne's determination waivered and Lacey nodded encouragingly and motioned for her to go on.

Feeling her part was played, Lacey walked back to her car and waited in the shadows as Ariadne climbed the steps then crossed the wide porch and timidly knocked on the front door. Seconds later, she heard her father's heavy footsteps coming down the hall from his study and she had begun to shake. The tall beefy girl looked very young with her shoulders hunched forward and her hands locked in front of her. Lacey could see her shaking and wondered if her legs would hold.

The Reverend opened the door and had not immediately recognized his beautiful daughter in the unkempt street-person on his porch. His lips tightened and the sour look on his face had made Lacey cringe and ache to run to the girl's defense. Knowing it would be the wrong thing to do, she had fervently prayed instead.

Escape from Gomorrah

On the porch, Ariadne had looked up at her father and begged: "Daddy...Daddy, can I come home? Please? I miss you and Mommy so much, please?" The Reverend had burst into tears and pulled his daughter into his arms kissing her over and over and shouting for Jane to come quickly because their baby was home. Satisfied that they would work it out from there, Lacey had driven away.

"I'm sorry, Lacey," he was saying. "I've prided myself on being an exceptional judge of character, but I never gave you a chance, *never* tried to get to know you. I couldn't see what a wonderful blessing it was to have you in my family. Please forgive me."

Sensing that he meant what he was saying, Lacey felt like a toxic spiritual jellyfish had been peeled off of her heart and relief loosed a flood of tears. The Reverend wept too and drew her onto his shoulder as they comforted and forgave each other.

Several minutes later, a third person entered the room. Thinking he had interrupted his father counseling a church member, Matthew would have slipped away if he had not recognized the keys on the bedside table. Very few people hugged his father and he could not bring himself to leave without finding out why his ex-wife was crying on the old man's shoulder.

While he waited, Matthew thoughtfully opened the box of Puffs. Lacey heard the cardboard popping and untangled herself from The Reverend's IV tubes as she wiped her face with the backs of her hands.

69

The Last Rose of Autumn

Resisting the urge to take her in his arms, Matthew handed her some tissues. She recognized his after-shave before her eyes cleared and apologized to him.

"I'm sorry, Matt, I didn't know you were coming or I'd have left sooner. I don't want to use up your visiting time."

"You don't have to go," he said gently touching her arm. "I hadn't planned on coming today, but about thirty minutes ago, I got a strong feeling I needed to be here. How long have you been here?"

Lacey looked at the clock. "Half hour."

"Dad!" he said sternly. "Did you have anything to do with this?"

"Yes," admitted his unintimidated father. "I asked Lacey to come so I could apologize to her. Then I prayed that if God wanted you here, you'd show up. I did you kids a great disservice by driving you apart and I apologize to you both. Please forgive me for being an old fool."

They talked for a long time and many wounds were healed. It's never all one person's fault; after The Reverend apologized, Matthew apologized for not being more understanding of his father's desires and for not spending enough time with his bride. In turn, Lacey admitted that she had been jealous of Matthew's relationship with his father and apologized for expecting her husband to meet needs only God could fulfill. The conversation flowed so easily that it made Lacey wonder why they could not have talked this way before.

Escape from Gomorrah

When they all had their say, The Reverend prayed then sleepily suggested that Matthew take Lacey out to get something to eat because her stomach was growling.

"Haven't you eaten?" he asked with genuine concern.

Behind Matthew's back, The Reverend coached Lacey by assuming a hang-dog expression and pouting out his bottom lip. When he shamelessly batted his eyelashes, the unexpected display of humor surprised a burst of laughter out of Lacey and Matthew held onto her arms and moved a little to block her view of his father.

"No coaching from the peanut gallery. Lacey, will you let me take you out to get some lunch?"

This made her laugh even more. The change in the father/son relationship was so refreshing that she had to compliment them.

"It's all thanks to you, my dear," admitted her former enemy. "We never would have gotten to this place without you. Go have your lunch and come back if you want. Jane and Ariadne will be here later and I know they would love to see you; but right now, I need a nap."

So they both kissed his cheek and picked up their keys. As they left, a very businesslike nurse came into the room carrying a tray of ominous-looking supplies.

In the hallway, Lacey gripped Matthew's arm and asked: "Is he going to die?"

"Sooooooner or later," Matthew replied giving her a puzzled look as he took advantage of the situation to take hold of her hand, "didn't he tell you why he's in here?"

"No, and I didn't want to ask."

Mischief twinkled in his eyes and he pulled her close so their shoulders touched as he whispered. "He was on a fishing trip and snagged himself in the rear with a hook. By the time he got back, it was infected."

Lacey stared at him for a moment then laughed until her sides hurt. "Oh no! How embarrassing for him."

"I know, isn't it great!" gloated The Reverend's adoring son as he basked in the poetic justice.

He pushed open the door for the woman he loved and guided her toward his car by sliding his hand around her waist and holding on. "Where would you like to go for lunch?"

"Kelly's," she answered without thinking that it was where they had gone on their first date. "I hear you sold your company," she remarked conversationally. "What are you going to do now? Got any plans?"

Mathew smiled enigmatically. A new, and unexpected, plan was forming in his mind, but it was a little early to tell if it would work out the way he wanted. But one thing he did know: going forward he would not make the same mistakes. This time, he would ask God to guide him instead

Escape from Gomorrah

of asking God to clean up behind him. And this time, however it turned out, he knew it would be better.

Something Pretty

'Oh honey,' thought the sales associate; 'you'll never get your plump little self into that size six. You're broader than I am, and I wear a fourteen.'

Out loud she confidingly informed the lady: "This season, the sizes from this manufacturer seem all mixed up. Some that are tagged sixteen look like eights! I'd just find one that fits and cut the size tag out when you get ready to wear it."

"Really!" gasped the customer thrilled to hear such unexpected inside information.

Of course it was not true. High-end department stores do not buy from labels that make those kinds of mistakes, but it made the lady feel better and she selected an arm full of dresses she might actually be able to wear and headed to the dressing room.

"There's probably a special place in hell for salespeople," mused the associate, then she rejected the possibility and silently asked God to forgive her for altering the truth instead of the dresses and added

Something Pretty

a request for Him to send her someone who *really* needed her help today. She was only mildly hopeful, but her prayer was about to be answered.

Two ladies walked into the dress department and began flipping through the racks. One was in her mid fifties and the other her mid twenties. Mother and daughter? No. Aunt and niece? No. Mother-in-law and daughter-in-law? Mmmmmh, no. Figuring out people was a game the associate played to make time pass more quickly and this pair intrigued her. Determined to satisfy her curiosity, she smiled and asked if she could help them find something. They declined so she continued to straighten the rack she was working on and pretended not to pay attention even though she could not help over hearing their conversation.

"What about this?" suggested the younger woman holding up a beaded dress with short sleeves and a low-cut neckline.

"Wrong color," answered the older woman. "What about this?"

"Too old, totally not Linda," said the younger woman.

Their conversation continued this way for about fifteen minutes as they wandered from rack to rack looking at dresses for the absent Linda and telling funny anecdotes that started with: "Do you remember the time she..."

The associate gathered that Linda was a fun character, someone who loved well and was well-loved

The Last Rose of Autumn

in return, the kind of person everyone wishes they had in their life. It sounded like she had lost a lot of weight and the associate wondered if the dress was a gift to celebrate or perhaps they just wanted their friend to have something that looked good on her. Whatever the reason, they were not having any luck and their jovial conversation had an odd tendency to lapse into heavy silences accompanied by wistful sighs. Judging it time to volunteer again, the associate asked if they were finding what they wanted.

The ladies exchanged bewildered looks and shrugged their shoulders. "Not really," said the younger woman. "We're looking for a dress for my aunt, who is her best friend, and we're not doing very well."

"Special occasion?" asked the associate thinking she would never have guessed the connection between the two shoppers.

Again the ladies looked at each other and hesitated as if they did not know how to respond. Finally the best friend looked squarely at the associate and said: "You could say that. Linda has end stage cancer and it's for her to be buried in. She asked us to get her something pretty."

'I was born for a time such as this,' thought the associate and she felt the presence of God come over her. "She must trust you a lot and I bet you feel a lot of pressure to get it right," she said with a gentle understanding that took both of the ladies by surprise.

Something Pretty

They were prepared for disbelief and shock, even rejection; they were not prepared for someone who had never met their beloved Linda to understand so completely. Both nodded wholehearted confirmation and the search for something pretty took a businesslike turn.

"Is she casual or dressy?" asked the associate.

"Definitely casual but she wants something nicer than what she normally wears," supplied the best friend. "Tee shirts and blue jeans won't do."

"What colors does she like?"

Both ladies answered in unison. "Bright!"

The niece clarified: "Happy colors: hot pink, red, turquoise, coral, lime green, pick your favorite tropical island post card, and that's Linda."

"What size?"

"Well, she used to be a plus, but she's down to around a hundred pounds," answered her old friend in a husky voice.

"I brought measurements," said the niece digging in her handbag and turning slightly away to give her companion time to recover.

"Does she have special jewelry that she wants to wear?" asked the associate.

"No, whatever she had, she's given away already."

"Okay, she needs a dress, long sleeves to cover her arms and cut high at the neck, pretty but not frilly, bright colored, and some great earrings to go with it."

The Last Rose of Autumn

"Yes!" exclaimed the niece wondering how someone could make it all sound so simple. "That's exactly it!"

The associate took the measurements from the niece, showed the ladies to some comfortable chairs and suggested that they take a seat while she organized a couple of ensembles.

She knew the store well and made fast work of the hunt. On her way back from the jewelry boutique, something on a sale rack in the lingerie department caught her eye. It was not part of her master plan, but the concept would work so she checked the size tag and added it to her collection.

Back in the dress department, she went to a rack near the ladies and quickly organized what she had gathered to present them with two options. The first was a turquoise suit with a coordinating blouse and a bold scarf to add color and flair.

"The colors are right," said the niece, but the little pucker between her eyebrows told the associate that this was not the right ensemble.

"Yes," agreed the best friend, "it works, but it looks like something you might wear to a job interview. I'm pretty sure she's got this gig."

Not discouraged, the associate hung the rejected suit on the far side of the rack and pulled forward the second option. Both ladies smiled. Cotton print dresses with lace bodices and high, tapered collar were very much in style, and the one she held was a bright fuchsia with tiny multi-colored flowers.

Something Pretty

The sleeves were long with lace cuffs, and a fabric belt that tied in the back would allow the dress to be tailored to Linda's decreasing size. It was feminine without being frilly. To complete the look, the associate held out two pairs of earrings and both ladies pointed to a pair of bold garnet posts that blended perfectly with the flowers in the fabric.

"That's it! That's the outfit. She'll love that..." whispered Linda's best friend as her eyes filled with sentimental tears. "She'll look so pretty..." and the younger woman leaned over the arms of the chairs to grasp her hand.

The sympathetic frog in her throat kept the associate from speaking, so she nodded and hung the dress on the end of the rack and handed the earrings to the niece who pressed them to her heart.

"Ahem, uh...we're not quite done," interrupted their hero with a mysterious smile as she turned to pull forward the item she had picked up in the lingerie department. "I know you don't need undies when you're buried, but I really think Linda should go out in style," and she showed them a knee-length black negligee. "Esther soaked in fragrant oil for a year and was dressed in the finest silks when she met the king. I think Linda deserves some silk too, how about this instead of a slip?"

The woman who had been Linda's best friend since they were crazy teenagers coughed then chuckled knowingly at some undisclosed memory and clamped her hand over her mouth as her eyes

The Last Rose of Autumn

twinkled wildly; the niece blinked a few times and tried to purse her lips in and look stern but could not sustain the pretense and burst out laughing.

"And," added the associate, "a little something for her tootsies." She brought her hand around from behind her back and revealed a pair of bubble-gum pink fuzzy bunny slippers.

"Perfect! Absolutely perfect!" celebrated the two women as they laughed and cried and hugged each other then the kind woman who had helped them.

"That was an odd couple, what were they up to?" asked one of the other sales associates as the ladies walked out of the store smiling.

"They came in to get something pretty for their friend to be buried in."

"Oh! That's bizarre!"

"No, that's love."

So often, we undervalue the every day things we do for the people God puts in our paths, but they don't come our way by accident. He gave each of us a particular personality with talents and gifts that make us who we are so we can share Him with the world. We are filled to be emptied again. *Whatever you do, do it as if you are doing it for God .*

You Can't Take it with You

Never were two brothers less alike. The younger brother, Horace, was a pompous little man with a purposeful stride and an exaggerated air of self-consequence. His barrel chest puffed out in front of him like a mating partridge, and when he spoke, his voice had a penetrating quality that assaulted the ears of the sensitive. One of the sensitive people most deeply aggrieved by Horace was his older brother Sherwin.

Quiet and thoughtful, Sherwin had an artist's soul and an engineer's mind. He liked intricate work and had spent his life making and repairing clocks and watches with an eye to detail that rivaled any Swiss watchmaker. His gentle disposition and stooped posture lent the appearance of frailty. This was an illusion. Sherwin neither argued nor acquiesced, but in his own peculiar way, he managed to get done

The Last Rose of Autumn

what he wanted to do while avoiding that which he would rather not do.

In spite of their differences, both brothers were benefactors of the community. One promoted business and commerce, the other made quiet contributions to individuals in need and worthy charities. While both were respected, the entrepreneur garnered accolades for his brains even though everyone knew that when he did something for the community, there was something even bigger in it for himself. The philanthropist was simply loved.

As a family, they spent little time together, their infrequent visits usually occurring when Horace's sense of duty prompted him to stop in, *if* he happened to be in the neighborhood. Sadly enough, every visit seemed to run the same course. Horace would burst into Sherwin's dusty little shop and loudly announce himself. Already summoned from the back by the soft tinkling of the bell on the door, the be-speckled shopkeeper would greet his sibling with mild affection, and they would have the same the conversation they had had for the past thirty years.

Horace would advise Sherwin to clean up the shop and modernize his displays and equipment. A man of means should present a more affluent appearance, spend a little money! After all, you can't take it with you.

Sherwin would smile the enigmatic smile of one not really paying attention and illusively reply: "We'll see."

82

You Can't Take it with You

Although he feigned disinterest, Horace itched to know the true nature of his brother's finances. It was not that he needed money, far from it. He was just nosy, a nosy acquisitive man who liked to manage other people's affairs, and he would justify his thoughts by reminding himself that he was his brother's heir.

Many nights he laid awake planning how he was going to spend the hypothetical wind fall he would inherit when his brother died. The clock maker's expertise brought him a great deal of work, but he lived modestly in two little rooms behind the shop and never traveled and rarely spent money on himself. Like his brother, Sherwin was single, but he was a widower. As for Horace, well, Horace had never married on purpose. The root cause of his bachelorhood being the fact that his parsimony led to a fear of alimony. When the time came to spend his brother's money, however much or however little there was, Horace would be spending it on himself.

Late one afternoon in the year of the dreary wet spring, the police chief rang to tell Horace that a customer had found Sherwin slumped over his worktable and his body had been taken to the funeral home. The Chief gave his condolences and asked if Horace would take the necessary clothes to the undertaker.

Horace nearly burst his buttons with anticipation, now was his chance! He had waited for years to discover the extent of Sherwin's wealth and the

The Last Rose of Autumn

Chief had just given him carte blanche to do so. He was so elated that he nearly forgot to act sorrowful. Catching himself, he artfully sniffed and thanked the Chief then hurried across town.

Sherwin's assets would be somewhere on the premises; the Great Depression had stripped away the clock-maker's early earnings and he had never overcome his distrust of banks. Horace entered the gloomy little building and shuddered. It had always seemed dismal to him, but now a coldness closed in around him and he felt uncomfortable being there alone. It was odd that he had never noticed how loudly the clocks ticked, and he disliked the empty echoing sound they made now that their owner was gone. They were machines, just machines, but he had the eerie feeling they were watching him.

Horace shook off his discomfort and quickly searched the cramped area behind the counter. The antique safe was not locked and it held only a small amount of cash. Surely there had to be more. A methodical search of the dressers and cupboards in the living area yielded nothing of value aside from a few small pieces of jewelry that had belonged to Sherwin's wife and some odds and ends—a gold watch chain, a couple of tie pins, and a few cufflinks.

There had to be more somewhere!

Tired of looking and fearful of being caught, Horace decided to end his search and come back another time. He had the right to be there, of course, but we judge others by ourselves and he worried that people would talk. He was a man of wealth and influence, he did not want anyone to get the idea that he was snooping. Then it occurred to him that the hands on the clock above the fireplace had not moved.

Indifferent to most things, Sherwin had been meticulous about clocks. Horace knew he would not have let one stand idle unless it served another purpose. With trembling hands and bated breath, Horace looked for a way to open it and discovered a clever door concealed in the back. It required a key and excitement sharpened his wits. He remembered a ring of keys laying on the worktable and tried one after another until the lock turned and the door could be opened.

Horace hesitated. What if it was empty? What if there was very little money in it? Sherwin had been a softhearted old fool forever giving money to the pathetic poor whom Horace despised. What if...?

Forcing himself to get a grip, he reasoned that whatever was in the clock was his and he had no thought of sharing it with the needy, the Internal Revenue Service, or anyone else. A slow cunning smile crept over his face and he pulled on the key. Stacked neatly where the clockworks should have been was a small fortune.

"Bless your frugal old soul!" he chuckled. How very kind of his dear brother to have saved so much money for him to enjoy. He found a brown paper bag and transferred the bills. Then he gathered up the threadbare suit and yellowed shirt Sherwin

The Last Rose of Autumn

would be buried in and prepared to leave the shop. He left the cash in the safe as he had found it and carefully locked the shop door so anyone who might be watching would know he was diligent.

At the funeral home, he realized he had forgotten to bring a necktie and thoughtfully removed his own and laid it with the clothes. It was silk and very expensive, but Horace had decided that it was not to his taste so parting with it was no sacrifice.

After Horace delivered the clothes to the undertaker, he went home to spend a very pleasant evening counting his brother's money and making plans. He even decided to buy Sherwin a nice headstone, the charming stacks of green having made him feel magnanimous.

The jeweler who enjoyed Horace's patronage was the soul of discretion. If he thought it odd to select a particularly fine diamond then have it set in a flower-shaped tie pin so only a small part of the center showed, he kept his thoughts to himself. Rich people frequently have eccentric ways and they do not appreciate prying questions.

While the diamond was being mounted, Horace drove to the stonemason's and selected a modest headstone. He might have chosen a more elaborate stone. He might have chosen a nicer quality stone or even a prettier font for the information that would be carved into it. Unfortunately, the diamond he purchased had cost more than anticipated. To salve his conscience he reasoned that Sherwin had always

You Can't Take it with You

been a humble man so there was no point in being extravagant now.

Two days later, a small group of mourners solemnly trekked up the hill to the cemetery. The graves were laid out on an unforgiving mound of sticky clay ribboned with sand, it was unpredictable to dig and hardened like concrete as it settled. The rain that had lasted for days had let up, but it seemed as if the heavens were grieving over Sherwin's death. The sky was dark and the air felt ladened as if it had not finished pouring out its sadness. Drenched blades of saw grass bowed close to the ground and tree limbs drooped as raindrops trembled and fell from their leaves like tears falling from eyelashes.

Everything seemed sad, everything but Horace that is. He briskly strode up the hill exquisitely attired in a new black suit, a crisp white shirt, and a dark gray tie. The deceptively modest diamond pin holding his tie in place looked quite appropriate for a funeral; and if his hand strayed to it more often than need be, anyone noticing correctly assumed that Horace was bored.

The pastor welcomed those gathered and gave a short heartfelt message honoring Sherwin's love for God and kindness to man. Then he politely, albeit regretfully, asked Horace if he would care to say a few words. Never one to pass up the opportunity to be the center of attention, he portentously went to stand beside the coffin. He placed his hand on the modest box that was suspended by ropes over the

The Last Rose of Autumn

deep hole waiting to receive it, and bowed his head for a moment making a great show of his insincere grief. Then he heaved a gusty sigh and started to turn so he could make his speech, but as he stepped, the ground gave way and Horace slithered under the coffin and fell into the grave.

His head collided with the coffin knocking it out of balance and the ropes holding it let out a searing shriek as the wooden box slid. It teetered, precariously ready to drop into the grave on top of the terrified man who cowered in the mud below with his arm thrown up in a pitiful attempt to protect himself from what might come. As the coffin swayed wildly on its ropes, slits of light bounced from side to side above him, and Horace wondered if he would get out of this pit or be buried alive under his brother.

The gravediggers and the mourners rushed forward and steadied the ropes then helped Horace clamber out. Afraid for them, the undertaker said to let go and the ground caved in on top of the coffin as the earth embraced Sherwin.

It was starting to drizzle again, so the pastor gave a quick benediction and the guests headed back to their cars. As they walked, the pastor considerately asked Horace if he was all right.

Al...alright? Why...why yes, he was alright, just a little muddy. But his laugh was forced and a queasy knot pushed at his Adam's apple.

Nervously brushing at the mud embedded in his clothes, Horace tried to regain his self-command,

You Can't Take it with You

but as his hand straightened his tie, an even sicker feeling gripped his chest. The clever diamond tie pin was gone. Brought to a standstill, he turned back only to see the gravediggers throwing the last few shovels of clay onto the grave and packing it down with the backs of their shovels.

The irksome chatter of a jay sheltering in a nearby tree seemed to mock: "You can't take it with you!"

And the wind softly sighed: *"We'll see..."*

Tom, the aged gardener who took care of Horace's estate was waiting for him at the bottom of the hill. He had been Horace's employee for nearly twenty years, but Horace barely recognized the man. He looked very different in his Sunday best. He was a regular churchgoer and Sherwin would have recognized him, but Horace did not recall ever having seen the man in anything other than green work clothes and an old cap. Without the cap, he saw that Tom was balding and that the white of his head stopped abruptly at his eyebrows where the dark tan of his skin testified to long hours spent outside. Over the years, weather and worry had etched deep lines around his eyes but Horace had never noticed.

The man held out a plaid blanket and timidly asked Horace if he would like to have it spread over the car seat as protection from the mud. Puzzled, Horace wondered why Tom acted afraid of him, then a series of memories played before his mind's eye. Horace saw himself. He saw how he had

The Last Rose of Autumn

treated the man. And he was shocked. He had been rude, demanding, and condescending. Why would someone he had abused so badly offer him kindness? To his further surprise, Tom opened the driver's side door and carefully tucked the blanket over the expensive leather seat and spread a newspaper on the floor to protect the carpet.

Ashamed and wanting to make amends, Horace extended his hand then started to draw it back in embarrassment as he realized how dirty he was, but he looked into Tom's eyes and saw only compassion. Tom held out his own callused hand saying that a little mud never hurt anyone, so Horace shook his hand for the first time and awkwardly thanked him for the use of the blanket.

Normally, Horace would have reached for his wallet and handed the man a few dollars for his efforts. He would not have looked in his eyes much less have shaken his hand, but the scales were falling from Horace's eyes.

He drove his luxury car to his opulent house where he unlocked the carved front door and mechanically wiped his custom-made shoes on the Persian rug he used as a doormat. He crossed the wide foyer and went into his formal living room. It was silent and dark but he did not turn on a lamp or open the drapes. He walked to an upholstered chair that he never used and sat down sightlessly staring in front of him. In the dim light, the vibrant colors of the lavishly decorated room looked gray; the emeralds and sapphires and deep golds in the fabrics could have been burlap. Horace did not see them.

He was thinking, thinking about what he had heard as he cowered in Sherwin's grave. He had not heard the shouts of the men above him, he had heard the ticking of his own clock. And in the dizzy sway of his brother's coffin, he had seen the pendulum swing of his own out-of-balance life. The voice that he *had* heard was not one of concern, but contempt.

"Fool! Who will spend your money when you're dead?"

How could a man who was so smart at business be so stupid at life? He felt that his heart was as hard as a rock and no bigger than a grain of sand. Then the voice he had heard in the cemetery spoke to him again saying that a grain of sand might be small, but it's mighty. In a motor, it would ruin the gears; in your eye, it would blind; rubbed on wood, it cut; but seeded into an oyster, it could become a pearl. And Horace knew that his life was about to change.

He pondered for a long time and came to some conclusions: primary of which was that his brother may have been soft-hearted, but he was no fool.

Horace went to his desk and wrote out several checks, each equal to the amount of money he had taken from Sherwin's clock; they were made out to Sherwin's church, the charities he had supported, and several worthy causes that served people in need. The next day, he was waiting in the kitchen when Tom's truck pulled in beside the garage, and

The Last Rose of Autumn

he stepped onto the wide veranda and called out inviting him to come in for coffee.

Tom stared in disbelief. He was not a young man and he momentarily feared that he was having a stroke or some other mind-altering medical crisis; but Horace smiled and waved so the gardener carefully wiped his boots on the grass and went inside.

Horace poured Tom a cup of coffee and motioned him to a chair at the kitchen table then sat down across from him and spoke what was on his mind. He knew Tom was Sherwin's friend, and Horace hoped he would understand as he talked about the vision he had seen in the grave and what the voice had said to him about sand. Then Horace asked: "Tom, do you think I'm crazy?"

Tom laughed and said that if he was, he sure had a lot of company.

Horace felt relieved and asked what to do next, so Tom led him in a little prayer that has huge results: "Jesus, I'm sorry for the things I've done. I believe you died for my sins, and I ask you to come into my life and be my lord and savior."

As Horace finished, something hard and mean in him broke; he released a choking sob then hung his head and cried. An overwhelming sense of peace filled him, and he knew that he was free from the chains of greed and pride that had held him captive.

Tom told him that Sherwin had prayed for him every day and that he would be very happy his little brother had accepted Christ. Then he prayed over

You Can't Take it with You

Horace asking God to lead him, teach him, and show him the path He wanted this new believer to take. Horace was sorrowful and deeply regretted the time he had wasted, but Tom patted his shoulder and told him not to worry. God would redeem the time and use everything in Horace's life to help somebody else. Yes, God *could* do that.

Later that day as Horace got his black suit ready to send to the cleaners, he noticed a clump of mud in one of the cuffs and shook it into the trash can. As it fell, his eye was attracted to something shiny in the dirt and he reached down to inspect it. Without thinking that he might ruin his manicure, he crushed the mud and it fell apart revealing the diamond tie pin he thought was lost. He stared at it in wonder and words ran through his head:

"I once was lost, but now I'm found, was blind but now I see."

Ohio Blue Tip

It didn't seem fair, it just didn't seem fair. Tomorrow afternoon at 2:30 Grandma would be laid to rest for all eternity beside the wrong man. It was not a clerical error, it was just life. Instead of being buried beside her second husband, the man who had brought happiness, wonderful adventures, and a Godly marriage to her, Grandma would be buried next to her first husband.

I never knew my real grandfather; he died when I was a baby, and the family rarely talked about him. The little I had heard gave me the opinion that Granddad had been a testy, nervous man with a waspish personality and wandering ways. He did not sound like the kind of man my grandmother deserved at all, and I often wondered if his loss had been felt with anything other than relief.

The year I turned six, Grandma had remarried, this time to a round little man from her church. He was warm and friendly, always smiling and pleasant,

Ohio Blue Tip

and his only vice was smoking a smelly little black pipe. My mom and my aunts discussed what to call this new person in their lives and had decided that since they already had a Dad, they would call their stepfather Pop. Considering his bubbly personality, I thought the nickname fit well.

Grandma and Pop were good together. For two people commonly thought to be past their prime, they sure enjoyed life traveling and visiting all over the country, sightseeing, and just having fun. And when they were home, their door was always open to their merged families. Visits to their house were special and I particularly remember one summer evening when the cousins had been playing outside after supper. It was getting dark and we had begged Grandma to come out and tell us a ghost story.

After a great deal of coaxing, she sat down on the porch steps and dried her hands on a flour sack dishtowel as she waited for us to seat ourselves on the grass at her feet. When we were settled, this God-fearing, pragmatic, little old lady proceeded to tell us a hair-raising tale that was calculated to give us nightmares for weeks. Near the end of her story, Grandma dramatically dropped her voice and peered off into the backyard directing our attention to an ancient tree shrouded in evening mist where the errant ghost was said to appear.

Then, just as we turned, Grandma shook the big white dishtowel she was holding in our faces and screamed like a banshee. We jumped and shrieked,

The Last Rose of Autumn

and as the kids in front tried to back away from the *ghost*, the rest of us fell over like dominoes. We laughed and laughed and it was hard to imagine that a woman with so much life was in her seventies.

Pop was just as lively but what I remember most about him were the things he always had with him. These included a silver coin from France that he carried as a reminder to pray for those who had fought in "The Big War"; his war was World War I. In the same pocket was a bone-handled pocketknife that he would flip open with one thumb and use to whittle interesting things or cut up apples. His back pocket always held a big red hanky that could be counted on to have a clean corner to dry young tears. And his shirt pocket held that stinky little black pipe, a small packet of tobacco, and several Ohio Blue Tip matches.

Pop always carried the large kitchen matches because he said his pipe was a contrary old thing and needed a big fire. I suspected that he enjoyed fiddling with the matches more than he enjoyed the pipe. He would light his pipe then take the unused matches left in his hand and whittle on them while he told a story about Jesus. He would end the story by handing you two pieces of match stick that would form a cross when you snapped them together, and he would ask if you would like to finish the cross and accept Jesus as your lord and savior. Pop said that when you accepted Jesus, your life was linked with Him through His death on the cross, and you would never be separated from God's love again.

Ohio Blue Tip

Most of the other grandchildren had prayed with Pop and clicked their little crosses together, but not me. Even as a child, I had a hard heart and I felt angry with God for the unhappiness in my life. I heard the stories and I believed the words, but I would not let go of my anger and accept Jesus as my savior.

"God won't give up on you," Pop would say, "and neither will your Grandma and me. Your cross will be here when you are ready to take it up and follow Him."

Grandma and Pop were happy together for many years before Pop's health gave out and he had slipped into a coma. He woke up briefly one afternoon and my aunt, who was sitting with him, took the hand he stretched out and held it tightly.

"This is the hand that shook the hand of the Lord!" he had whispered returning her grasp. Then he had drifted away again.

Two days later he died. Everyone missed him terribly, but Grandma had said that one mustn't put on a long face when the Master called a faithful servant home. So we sang his favorite songs and dried our eyes, and life moved on.

That was twenty years ago, and now, the Master had called another faithful servant home. Standing beside her casket, I looked around at the beautiful flowers sent by people who loved her and wished things were different. I wished that somehow it could have been possible for Pop and Grandma to be buried side-by-side but knew it wasn't going to

The Last Rose of Autumn

happen. He had been buried beside his first wife, and Grandma's name had been carved on the gray granite stone next to Granddad's for decades. Some things are written in stone.

Soon family and friends would be coming to pay their last respects, but for now, the large visiting room was vacant except for me and the rows of empty chairs that silently stood vigil. I had come early to share one last moment alone with Grandma and to remember. As I looked at her peaceful face, I absently reached down to straighten the pleated lining that surrounded her. I tried to smooth the fabric but something under the folds kept them from laying flat. Perplexed, I felt around and pulled out a worn matchbox with a faded label that read "Ohio Blue Tip".

I slid the box open. Inside, nestled in an old red hanky were a silver coin worn smooth with age, a bone handled pocketknife, a smelly little black pipe, and two pieces of whittled-on match-stick that would form a cross when you clicked them together

I didn't need a letter to tell me those were the matches that would make my cross. And I didn't need a story from one of God's faithful servants to remind me that Christ's love would fill my heart and take away my anger and sadness. And I didn't need to see Him to know that the Holy Spirit was there waiting for me to just say yes...so I did.

And as I knelt to pray, I thanked them: Grandma and Pop, but most of all God, for never giving up on me.

Reference

Mr. Henry
Spare the rod—Proverbs 14:24
Thy rod and thy staff—Psalm 23:4
Do not provoke—Ephesians 6:4
Work out your own salvation—Philippians 2:12
This and more will you do—John 13:13-14

A Funny Thing Happened Today
No greater love—John 15:13

Birdhouses
David and Jonathan—1 Samuel 18:1
Iron sharpens iron—Proverbs 27:17
Deep calls to deep—Psalm 42:7
Armor bearers—1 Samuel 14:7
Chop a hole in the roof—Mark 2:2-4

A Shirt for Joe
I can do all things—Philippians 4:13

Escape From Gomorrah
Strengthened himself in God—1 Samuel 30:6
I can do all things—Romans 8:28
For He shall give his angels—Psalm 91:11-13
Look back—Genesis 19:26

Something Pretty
Time such as this—Esther 4:14
Whatever you do—1 Corinthians 10:31

You Can't Take It With You
Fool, then who will—Luke 12:20
Redeem the time—Ephesians 5:16

Ohio Blue Tip:
For God so loved the world that He gave His only begotten son that whoever believes in Him should not perish but have everlasting life.--John 3:16

CPSIA information can be obtained at www.ICGtesting.com
Printed in the USA
LVOW12s1217190713

343725LV00001B/1/P